BUG
PALS

AND OTHER FRIENDSHIP STORIES
Compiled by the Editors
of
Highlights for Children

Compilation copyright © 1995 by Highlights for Children, Inc.
Contents copyright by Highlights for Children, Inc.
Published by Highlights for Children, Inc.
P.O. Box 18201
Columbus, Ohio 43218-0201
Printed in the United States of America

ISBN 0-87534-650-2

Highlights is a registered trademark of Highlights for Children, Inc.

BUG
PALS

CONTENTS

BUG
PALS

By Janet S. Anderson

All afternoon Susan sat outside, waiting.

"Are you waiting for a cookie?" asked Mrs. Cable, Susan's good friend and next-door neighbor. "Here's one, fresh from the oven."

Susan shook her head. "No thanks. I'm just waiting for my father. There's his van now!" He turned into the driveway, and Susan ran up to him. "Is she in there? Did you bring her?"

"Sure did," said her father. Opening the back of the van, he pulled down a ramp. Then he pushed at a little box that hung on a cord around his neck. Very slowly, something rolled down onto the driveway and stopped.

It was a robot about the same height as Susan. It had arms and hands, but instead of legs it had wheels. From its square head gleamed the brightest green eyes Susan had ever seen.

Mrs. Cable was surprised. She came down from her porch to see, too. "Oh, my," she said.

"Ladies," said Susan's father, "meet Roberta."

"Hello, Roberta," said Susan.

Roberta's eyes flashed purple. "Hello, Sisan," she said. Her voice was squeaky and came from a small round grill in her chest. "We're going to be bug pals."

"What?" said Susan. "My name is *Susan,* and I don't like bugs."

Her father laughed. "Roberta means *big* pals. She gets her i's and u's mixed up. Let me show you how she works."

He showed Susan all the buttons on the little box. "Now, just remember. In lots of ways Roberta is smart, but sometimes she'll make mistakes. Be patient and you'll have fun together."

Susan looked again at the buttons. One turned on Roberta's "brain" so she could function. Another turned on her motor so she could move. One turned on her microphone so she could talk. Now the buttons all glowed bright red.

"Would she like a cookie?" asked Mrs. Cable.

Roberta's eyes flashed purple again. "Thank yoi," she said, "bit no. A cookie might make crimbs unsude of me."

"Crimbs?" said Mrs. Cable. "Unsude?" She backed away. "I don't understand. There's something wrong with that robot." She hurried down the driveway and into her house.

"Why dud she rin away?" said Roberta. "Why doesn't she luke me, Sisan?" Her eyes, green again, no longer glowed. They flickered dully.

"She'll like you," said Susan. "She just doesn't know you yet. Now, what do you like to play?"

Roberta's eyes flashed a happy purple. "Ball, Sisan. U love to play ball."

Susan got a beach ball from the garage. She threw it to Roberta. *Pssst* . . . Roberta's hard fingers punched holes in the thin plastic. In a minute all the air had oozed out, and the ball was ruined.

"Oh, Sisan," said Roberta. "That's awful. U dudn't thunk. U never thunk."

"Oh, that's OK, Roberta," said Susan. "It was an old ball. Come on. We'll do something else."

But with wheels, Roberta couldn't play hopscotch. She couldn't jump rope. She couldn't even climb Susan's favorite tree. Her eyes got duller and duller as one thing after another failed.

"That's all right," Susan kept saying. "It doesn't matter, Roberta."

But it did matter. What good was a playmate who couldn't play? At dinnertime Susan sadly shut Roberta off and left her standing next to the porch.

"Having fun with Roberta?" asked her father as they sat down.

"No," said Susan, "she can't talk right, and she can't play anything fun. She just stands there looking sad."

"Well, don't give up on her." said her father. "You'll find a way to talk and to play. You'll think of something. Think!"

So all through dinner Susan thought. She thought of all the things that she liked to do, and she thought of Roberta. As she ate her dessert, Susan started to smile. As soon as she'd finished, she got some things from the basement and hurried outside. Roberta was still standing there, quiet and sad.

"Roberta," said Susan, pushing her buttons, "Please forgive me. I've been dumb. Look!"

She showed Roberta the baseball she'd brought from the basement. "You can't hurt this ball, Roberta. It's hard. And look at this long rope. We'll tie one end to the mailbox, and you can turn the other end while I jump. We both can chant a jump rope rhyme. It'll be fun!"

Roberta's eyes flashed a hopeful purple. "And can we play hopscotch? And clumb your tree?"

"Sire!" said Susan. "I mean, sure! You can draw the hopscotch and throw, and I'll jump for both of us. And when I climb my tree, we'll hang a bucket on the rope and send each other messages. And we can roller-skate and have marching bands and play tag. And when it rains we can play rummy and dominos . . ."

Roberta started twirling around in excitement. "Rimmy! Domunos!" Suddenly, she stopped short. Mrs. Cable from next door was standing in front of her. She had two cookies. She also had a soft cloth and a can of metal polish.

"Susan," she said with a smile, "these cookies are for you. Roberta, what would you say to a nice bit of polishing?"

"Yupee!" said Roberta. "U'd love ut! And next tume yoi bake, call on me. U love to mux batter."

Mrs. Cable thought for a moment and then answered slowly. "Next tume U wull," she said.

And when she'd finished polishing and Susan had finished her cookies and Roberta had finished one final twirl of happiness, they all played red lught, green lught until bedtume.

11

The
Fort
in the
Bushes

By Judith A. Enderle

Davie and Sean were best friends. Ever since they could remember, they had lived next door to each other. They even had a secret door in the fence between their yards. Now Sean's family was moving. Sean's dad had a new job in Nebraska.

"Remember when we built our fort in the bushes in my yard?" Sean asked as he and Davie waited for the moving van to arrive.

"Yeah," said Davie. "Mr. McGee gave us some leftover lumber and an old doorknob."

"I wonder if the new people would mind if you moved the fort to your yard, Davie?"

"No. It wouldn't be the same without you to share it."

"How many secret passwords do you remember? The first one was 'peanuts,'" Sean said.

"Then my little sister found out, and we changed it to 'lightning.' And then, when we started third grade, we thought 'ten-four' would be better."

"Yeah, 'ten-four,'" Davie repeated sadly.

"I'll write you, Davie," Sean promised. "Besides, you might like the new kids that are moving in."

"I'll hate the new kids!" said Davie emphatically.

The moving van arrived and all too soon was packed. Sean gave Davie his newest puzzle book. Davie gave Sean his best marble with the red and blue swirls in it.

"Well, see you," said Sean. He ran for the car before Davie could see the tears in his eyes.

"Write," called Davie. He swallowed hard, but the lump in his throat didn't move. He waved until the car was out of sight.

For the next few days Davie moped around the house.

"Why don't you go down to the park?" suggested his mother. "You'll probably see some of the kids from school."

"Don't feel like it," Davie said.

"Play cards with me," said his sister, Sherrie.

"Not now," Davie said.

On Thursday when Davie came home from school, there was another moving van parked in the driveway by Sean's house.

I wish that meant Sean's family had changed their minds, thought Davie. But he knew they hadn't. Davie stopped to watch as chairs, lamps, boxes, and beds were unloaded and carried into the house. He noticed two bikes propped near the garage. He hurried home.

"The new family has moved in," said his mother. "Did you see them?"

"I saw their things being unloaded from the moving van," Davie answered.

"They have a girl, Darlene, almost Sherrie's age and a boy, Herbie, your age," said his mother.

"Oh," Davie mumbled.

"Why don't you stop over after school tomorrow and get to know them? Herbie and Darlene will be starting classes on Monday."

"I'll be busy."

"Davie," said his mother, "I know you miss Sean, but put yourself in Herbie's place. He doesn't know anyone here yet. You could make it much easier for him."

"I'll be busy," repeated Davie. "I have alot of homework to do after school."

His mother sighed, then she said, "A letter came for you today. It's on your dresser."

"I'll bet it's from Sean!" Davie shouted. He raced up the stairs two at a time, then ripped open the envelope that had been propped up on his dresser. It was postmarked Omaha, NE. It said:

Dear Davie,

How are you? I'm fine, I guess. Our new house is OK. I have a big room with built-in shelves. I haven't made any new friends yet. There are two little girls next door. I hope I meet some nice kids at school, but I'm kind of scared because I don't know if they will like me. I know I'll never have another friend as good as you. My new address is on the envelope. Please write back soon.

Your friend,
Sean

P.S. Hope that the kids at my old house know how lucky they are to live by you. They won't have to worry about making friends.

"I still hate the new kids," Davie muttered as he slipped the letter back into its envelope.

On the weekend, Davie saw the new kids in their yard and then later riding their bikes out front. His sister went next door and was soon playing with Darlene.

"Don't you want to get acquainted?" Davie's father asked.

Davie shook his head. He climbed a tree, carrying the puzzle book that Sean had given him. Herbie was in the yard next door. Davie could hear him talking with his dad.

"Why don't we just tear this thing down and build a better one, Herbie?"

Davie listened carefully.

"No way, Dad! This fort is great. It's just like the one Pete and I had at our old house."

"Speaking of Pete, have you met the boy next door? I saw him around earlier. His folks said he's in fourth grade, too. His name is Davie."

"Maybe tomorrow. He won't be like Pete. Pete will always be my best friend. I wish he could have moved with us."

Davie thought about what he had heard. He thought about Sean and the letter. He climbed down from the tree. He pushed the loose board in the fence that was a secret door.

"Hi," he said. "I'm Davie."

"Hi. I'm Herbert, but call me Herbie."

"My best friend, Sean, used to live here," Davie said. "We built the fort over there in the bushes."

"It's cool. My best friend, Pete, and I had one at my old house, but our fort's door didn't have a doorknob. We had to pull on an old piece of rope to open it. I've got a rug we could put inside if you want."

"OK, let's see how it looks," Davie said. "We have to think of a good password, too. It will be a secret from our sisters."

Give Your Wish a Chance

By Jay Stanton

Sharon's eyes opened wide and her breath almost stopped when she saw the white horse on the Nelsons' front porch. Its head and one leg were raised in a prancing motion, and the carved tendrils of the mane made Sharon want to twine her fingers around the curly ends. One blue glass eye seemed to wink, inviting her to come closer.

She took a step toward the Nelsons' house and stopped. The Nelsons were elderly people whose children had left home. Sharon was sure they didn't want children playing on their porch, even though they always gave her a cheery "hello" if they were in the garden when she walked by.

Sharon ran to her friend Andrea's house. When her friend opened the door, Sharon was gasping for breath and talking all at once. "Guess what, Andrea! There's a wonderful merry-go-round horse on the Nelsons' porch!"

Andrea's dark eyes glowed. "Good! Let's go ride it. We can pretend to be captives escaping a wicked witch."

They were the same age, but happy-go-lucky Andrea always seemed to take charge and run things her way. *Why can't I be like that?* Sharon wondered. Yesterday Miss Woods had named Ben class librarian when Sharon wanted it more than anything. She had turned away without speaking, hoping no one saw her tears.

She said aloud, "I know that we can't play on the Nelsons' porch."

"How do you know without asking? Michael says it never hurts to ask, as long as you're polite." Michael was Andrea's twelve-year-old brother, and he gave her lots of advice.

"What if they say no?"

"So it's no," shrugged Andrea. "At least we'll know we tried."

Andrea's black braids swished as she shook her head. "You ask. They know your parents better than they do mine. And besides," she teased, "you need the practice. You'd be class librarian if you'd spoken up yesterday. Miss Woods didn't know you wanted it."

Sharon almost snapped that since she, Sharon, had seen the horse first, Andrea should ask, but a thought stopped her. Perhaps Andrea was putting her on the right track. At least she would have Andrea with her.

They set off for the Nelsons' house. The prospect of knocking on the door and asking to ride the horse made a solid, cold lump in Sharon's stomach. Her mouth felt dry.

"Don't look so scared," said Andrea. "Keep thinking of the fun we'll have."

The lump didn't go away.

At the Nelsons' house Sharon's feet slowed, but Andrea tugged her arm. Sharon moved her feet to keep up with Andrea—almost. She felt ashamed of being afraid, always holding back, but what could she do about it? She stopped. "It makes me feel funny to ask somebody for something."

"Why feel funny? Anyone has a right to ask." Andrea folded her arms and looked hard at Sharon. "Sometimes you have to nudge your wishes."

Sharon's puzzlement must have shown.

Andrea explained. "Figure it this way. You want to ride someone else's horse, but if that someone doesn't know, your wish doesn't have a chance. If you ask, there's a chance that someone will say yes. Some chance is better than no chance, isn't it?"

Put that way, it's worth trying, thought Sharon. The lump didn't exactly go away, but now, as she looked at the door, it was a fluttery, excited feeling—fun in a strange kind of way, like a tickle, and a lot nicer than being scared stiff.

She combed her bangs with her fingers and patted the pink ribbon. She made a smile and held it all the way up the walk, the porch steps, and while Andrea pressed the doorbell.

When Mrs. Nelson opened the door, the smile was so set that Sharon could barely form words. Her memory prodded—*some chance is better than no chance.* "Hello, Mrs. Nelson," she quavered.

Tiny Mrs. Nelson wore a big checkered shirt over loose gardening pants, which made her look like a floppy little scarecrow. Her smile was bright and friendly.

Sharon pushed on. "My friend and I . . ." She started again. "My friend, Andrea de Silva, and I wondered if you would let us ride your merry-go-round horse."

Mrs. Nelson turned and called into the house. "Sam, we have some customers for your horse!"

Mr. Nelson appeared at the doorway carrying a newspaper. He was tall and slim, with a shiny bald head. "I thought Champion would bring us some visitors. Who wants to be first?"

Sharon was so pleased with the result of her courage that she didn't mind when Andrea raced over to Champion and patted his wooden nose. "He's beautiful!"

Andrea put her hands on the horse's back, leaped lightly, and sailed into the saddle. "I'm Paul Revere," she cried, "riding to warn the Minutemen. Haloo! To arms! To arms!"

She jiggled importantly in the saddle and rattled the reins. Then she reared back stiffly. "Whoa, Champion!" She threw a winning smile at Mr. Nelson. "Now, who shall I be?"

Before Mr. Nelson could answer, Sharon moved to Champion's side. "It's my turn now. I'll help you down."

Sharon was a Pony Express rider carrying the mail across the plains of Nebraska. Later, riding together, the girls pretended to be prisoners escaping the wicked queen of an icy planet.

Mr. and Mrs. Nelson appeared to enjoy the rides just as much as Andrea and Sharon did.

Afterwards, as they parted at the end of the Nelsons' walk, Andrea sighed. "Wow! That was fun! And just think, the Nelsons said we can come back again." She winked. "Thanks a lot for inviting me."

Sharon grinned. "Thanks for pushing me into it."

Make Lemonade

by Dorothy Brandt Marra

Skeeter Brown slouched along the wintry street. The February cold bit through his coat and set his bones chattering.

"What a day for a birthday," he muttered to himself, a scowl creasing his face. He slipped and slid down the icy hill to the back door of his building.

He pushed open the door to the high-rise apartment building where he lived and stomped into the hallway. Somehow it didn't seem fair to have a birthday in February. Nobody would remember it was his birthday. Everyone was worried about the weather and tired of winter.

"Hi, Skeeter," a voice called.

Skeeter looked up. Mr. Gurley, the apartment building supervisor, was tacking a big sign to the bulletin board.

"Hi," Skeeter answered.

"Here's something for you to do," Mr. Gurley said, pointing to the sign.

PARTY <u>TONIGHT</u>
**FOR ALL CHILDREN IN
THIS BUILDING!
7 P.M.
WEAR OUTDOOR CLOTHING**

Skeeter was puzzled. When he turned to ask about it, Mr. Gurley was gone. Skeeter paused for a moment, then decided to run to the grocery store across the street where his mother worked. He wanted to see if she knew anything about the party.

When he opened the door to the store, the smell of spices and olives greeted Skeeter. It was an old-fashioned store where dried foods were in bins and green olives floated in stone crocks. His mother smiled brightly.

"That sounds like fun," she said when Skeeter told her about the party.

"But whose party is it?" Skeeter asked softly, trying to hide his disappointment. "It's *my* birthday."

His mother stepped out from behind the counter and gave Skeeter a hug.

"Of course it is, Skeeter," she said. "We'll celebrate at dinner. Then you can go to the building party."

Skeeter trudged home, feeling worse than ever. Life just wasn't fair. Some kids had all the luck. They got to have parties. Skeeter felt very sad.

When he went into his building, he saw Mr. Gurley again. This time he was carrying a box with lemons in it.

"You look glum, Skeeter," he said. "Cheer up."

"It's not fair," Skeeter mumbled. "It's my birthday, but nobody cares."

"What makes you think nobody cares?" Mr. Gurley asked. "Your mother cares. I care. Happy Birthday!"

"Thanks."

But it didn't make Skeeter feel any better.

"You know," Mr. Gurley said, "when life gives you a lemon, make lemonade."

"What?" Skeeter asked.

Mr. Gurley took a lemon from the box and handed it to Skeeter with a smile.

"Here. Make lemonade."

Skeeter took the lemon. He was so completely puzzled that he forgot to thank Mr. Gurley or say good-bye. Staring at the lemon, he took the elevator up to his apartment.

Skeeter used the lemon to make two glasses of lemonade. He and his mother drank it with their dinner. His mother thought it was delicious.

"Mr. Gurley said that when life gives you a lemon, you should make lemonade," Skeeter told her.

His mother laughed.

"It's an old expression," she explained. "It means that even when things in life are sour, as sour as lemons, you can make the best of them. Add a little sugar and you'll get something that is really tasty—lemonade."

Skeeter sipped his lemonade, not sure he understood. His mother gave him a new winter coat and a book and a puzzle. He was starting to feel better now. Maybe the party would be fun.

At seven o'clock he went down to the community room. It was filled with chattering children. They were dressed in winter clothing. Mr. Gurley was standing beside a stack of flattened cardboard boxes. He blew his whistle and everyone in the room stopped talking.

"See these boxes?" he asked. "I flattened them and you can use them for sleds. The slope in back of the building has lots of good snow. You know, I used a box for sledding when I was a kid."

"Why?" someone asked.

"Because I never had a real sled," Mr. Gurley answered. "And a box is better anyway. No runners to dig down into the snow."

Mr. Gurley handed out the boxes. Most of them were empty paper-towel cartons. Skeeter took his and gave Mr. Gurley a smile.

"Is this like the lemon, Mr. Gurley?" Skeeter asked. "You make the best of what you have?"

"You've got it now, Skeeter!" Mr. Gurley said.

Skeeter and his friends whooped, yelled, and slid on the snow until their noses were as cold as the night air and their feet were as stiff as their frozen cardboard sleds.

A shrill blast on Mr. Gurley's whistle told them it was time to come in. They hurried into the warm community room, glad to be back inside.

But the room was changed! Twisted crepe paper hung in festive loops from the ceiling. Stacks of paper plates and cups formed neat rows on a table, next to hot dogs and buns. Roasting sticks were piled in front of the fireplace, where blazing wood crackled and popped.

On a table in the middle of the room was a big cake that said HAPPY BIRTHDAY, SKEETER!"

"Surprise!" everyone shouted.

Some of Skeeter's best friends had gifts for him. Skeeter caught his breath, unable to speak. People did care! He saw his mother, all aglow, standing beside the cake. Behind her, Mr. Gurley was stirring something in a big pitcher.

"Guess what we're having to drink," Mr. Gurley said with a twinkle in his eye.

"Lemonade!" Skeeter shouted.

A Best-Friends Smile

By Alesa M. Penso

Margaret Brandon was glad to be going to school today. "I'm all ready for the spelling test," she said to her friend, Karen. "I'm going to get a hundred again and keep my name on the Perfect Spellers chart."

"You always do," said Karen. This was the second year that they had been best friends. They swung their lunch boxes and walked with their special step. "Walk, two, three, and a skip."

When they got to school, Mr. Woodley had a surprise for them. "Class, we have a new student.

Her name is Julie Abbott. I hope that you'll all make her feel at home."

Everyone turned to stare at the new girl. She had beautiful curly hair, the kind that Margaret had always wished for herself, and she was wearing nice clothes.

"Karen, please take Julie under your wing for the day," said Mr. Woodley. "Show her around during recess and sit with her at lunch until she gets to know everyone." Karen nodded enthusiastically and smiled at Julie. Somehow the smile made Margaret feel left out.

When it was time for recess, Margaret took her usual place at the head of the line. Mr. Woodley always arranged the students alphabetically. But Mr. Woodley took Julie by the hand and placed her in front of Margaret. "Time for a change, Margaret," he said. "Julie's last name comes before yours in the alphabet. She'll be leading the line from now on."

Margaret tried to hide her disappointment. She knew that Julie couldn't help what letter her last name started with. But that made it no easier to march behind her all the way to the playground.

At the playground Margaret raced to the foursquare court, where she and Karen always met. Then she noticed Karen walking with Julie.

They had their heads close together, as if they were sharing secrets. They seemed to be giggling. Margaret wondered what they were whispering about. She felt very much alone. Suddenly recess was no longer any fun. She felt her stomach clamping into a knot.

Lunchtime was no better. Julie led the line to the cafeteria. She sat opposite Karen. They spoke in low voices so that Margaret couldn't hear. Margaret had a hard time finishing her sandwich, even though it was roast beef, her favorite.

The last lesson for the day was spelling. Margaret quickly looked over the spelling list. Last night she had memorized every word. But now her stomach didn't feel quite right. And every time she looked at Julie, she felt even worse. She tried hard not to think about Julie while Mr. Woodley called out the spelling words.

Mr. Woodley corrected the test papers. The class was quiet. Finally he rose from his desk, smiling. "Well, this is a surprise," he said. Margaret's mouth went dry. "We have a new Perfect Speller. Julie was the only student to get a hundred this week."

Margaret shut her eyes as Julie's name went up on the chart. Her own name came down for the first time all year. Margaret wanted to cry but was afraid the other children would see her. "OK, class is dismissed," said Mr. Woodley. "And don't feel bad, Margaret," he added quietly. "Everyone makes a mistake once in a while."

Margaret left school in defeat. She wasn't really surprised to see Julie walking beside Karen. Some best friend Karen was!

"Aren't you coming?" yelled Karen. "Julie's invited us both over to her house for cookies." They stopped and waited for Margaret.

Margaret scuffed her feet in the dust. She wasn't so sure that she wanted to eat any of Julie's cookies. All she wanted was for everything to be like before—before Julie came!

"My best friend in Colorado was named Margaret," Julie said to Karen. "I really miss her a lot. I didn't want to move away, but because of Dad's promotion we didn't have a choice." Her voice was trembly. She sounded as sad as Margaret had been after the spelling test.

Suddenly Margaret wondered what it would be like to leave her friends. What if the children in a new school didn't like her, especially being such a good speller? Perhaps there were other things they might not like about her, things she couldn't help.

Quickly, Margaret made her decision. She ran and caught up with Julie and Karen. She barged between them and linked her arms in theirs.

Julie looked surprised. Then she confided, "Margaret, we did that spelling list last week in my old school. And last week I missed two words."

Margaret started to giggle. She felt the tightness in her stomach begin to relax. "Julie, let me show you how we do our special step on the way home every day."

Margaret and Karen gave each other their best-friends smile. The smile was easily big enough to include Julie. "Walk, two, three, and a skip."

P.V.
and the
Sparrow
Lady

By Sandra Soli

She was quite old. Nobody knew whether she had ever had children, or how she had ended up in that big house alone. She'd nod as she passed, walking two blocks for groceries. Her name was Olive Jasper, but you'd have to think a moment to come up with the name. Most everybody called her the Sparrow Lady.

Sun or snow, she fed the birds; never missed a day, even at Christmas. You could always tell when the Sparrow Lady was restocking the bird pantry, because on those days she wheeled home a grocery cart borrowed from Mr. Yu's store, filled with bags of millet and sunflower seeds. The cart stayed parked by her front gate until the next shopping trip.

Next door to Mrs. Jasper lived a kid named P.V., who knew a lot about the neighborhood because he paid attention to things. P.V. and the Sparrow Lady were not actually friends, not at first. In the winter she'd ask him to carry birdseed sacks from the grocery cart to her backyard, where he would dump seed into a large plastic trash can on the patio. She paid him fifty cents a bag, and usually there were two.

Otherwise he didn't see much of her. His mother said, "P.V., it's rude to spy on neighbors, and you are not to insult her by asking if she needs anything. She doesn't. She likes to look after herself."

But P.V. tried to watch out for Sparrow Lady in ways that he could. He liked being her neighbor. The hug she always had ready was even better than the money she paid him, but he had to admit that her oatmeal cookies were terrible—they tasted like pieces of gravel stuck together.

"Have one of these, P.V. The birds love them." He always thanked her and said he would save it for later.

P.V. worried about Sparrow Lady sometimes. On the way to school he'd look to see if her curtains were open. Each afternoon he'd peek in her mailbox to be sure she had been out there.

On Halloween night somebody egged her front door. P.V. felt bad that he hadn't seen or heard anything. He helped her clean up the mess for free. He could see that Sparrow Lady sorrowed over it, but there wasn't much he could do.

He began making daily visits after school. P.V. helped clean out the birdbath and fill it with fresh water from the garden hose. Sparrow Lady talked to him about living with birds.

"It's something, having all these creatures depend on you," she said. She told P.V. that birds carry their own special powers, and that sometimes men have taken names from birds so that they can borrow some of that power: Black Crow, War Eagle, Lone Hawk.

"It's a shame that these little ones get no attention, though," Sparrow Lady told him. "You'd be surprised to know how many varieties of sparrows there are."

She showed P.V. their pictures in a bird book: the chipping sparrow, the field sparrow with his bright pink bill, the fat and funny swamp sparrow, always shy and generally tucked under a bush, keeping to himself. So many sparrows! P.V. found himself paying more attention to birds, testing himself to see which ones he could recognize.

Although several feeders decorated Sparrow Lady's sycamore tree, P.V. noticed that the large birds didn't use them much. Flame-red cardinals and a few finches were faithful customers, and sometimes a pair of rowdy, screeching blue jays. When jays bullied the other birds, Sparrow Lady chased them with an orange fly swatter and a loud whoop.

P.V. could see that Sparrow Lady liked the small, ordinary birds best. They twittered their thanks as they savored her gift of seed. Their favorite treat was chunks of French bread left from supper the night before. The sparrows had a good life; she saw to it.

One afternoon Sparrow Lady told P.V. about her secret wish. Her eyes brightened in the telling. "Oh, P.V., wouldn't it be a great life, learning sky songs, soaring through the air on feathered wings."

She held up the fingers of both hands, spreading them wide open to feel the wind dance through. Surely it was possible, she said, by studying the birds long enough. You'd just step forward firmly, lean into it a bit, and then think yourself right on up there.

"I know I could make it as far as the light pole," she said. "Wouldn't that shake up everyone in the neighborhood!"

A few months later, on a sunny Saturday, Sparrow Lady knocked at P.V.'s door, something she'd never done before even though by now they were good friends. P.V. was amazed. His mother asked what was the matter, hurrying to get coffee for their visitor.

"Everything's fine," said the Sparrow Lady, "but I couldn't wait for P.V. today. So much to do." She flapped her arms excitedly. "I'm taking a trip in a few days. By air," she added.

P.V. was surprised to hear these travel plans. He'd never known her to be gone a single day in his entire life.

"Oh, Sp—I mean, Mrs.—uh, Jasper," P.V. stammered. "You mean you're going to take a trip all by yourself?"

"P.V., honey, I've been thinking about this for a long time," she said. "I had to get up the courage to do it. So, I'm doing it. Be happy for me. Besides, I won't be all by myself, you know."

"OK," said P.V. "But where are you going?"

"Here and there," replied Sparrow Lady. "Everywhere! Lots of grand places. Now, listen. I want you to see to the birds while I'm gone. I know you can be trusted." Leaning close to P.V.'s ear, she spoke gently. "P.V., you're a good friend. The birds know it. I promise, you don't have to worry about me anymore.

"Take care of yourself," she said with a hug. "You're a fine boy. I know you can take care of things." And Sparrow Lady went home.

P.V. watched her cross the driveway. His mouth felt stuck open. After a talk with his mother, he felt no better. "She's entitled to a vacation, P.V. Don't fret yourself. All you have to do is feed the birds for her. The responsibility will be good for you."

But P.V. missed Sparrow Lady already, even though he knew the trip was important to her. He waited for Sparrow Lady to depart, squinting through the kitchen curtains for a glimpse of activity next door. Nothing. In the middle of the night he thought he heard something, but when he ran to the window, all he saw was the streetlight gleaming on the sidewalk.

As it happened, even spying didn't work. P.V. missed the whole thing. Sparrow Lady left the neighborhood on a Thursday morning. Perplexed neighbors found her brown shoes placed neatly, side by side, at the mailbox. Birds were carrying on fiercely, perched on telephone wires for miles, like question marks.

In no time the house was sold. A new family came to occupy Sparrow Lady's house. They had *cats*. The sparrows had a general fit, then took off.

P.V. liked to think the birds caught up with her. He wondered if she was having fun traveling the world, swooping over cities and mountains with her arms out to the wind. What a funny sight she'd be, with no shoes on!

Nobody would believe him, of course, so P.V. kept the truth to himself. But he knew she had finally done it.

Just think of it—flying!

The Mississippi Move

By Cheryl Byler Keeler

They were sitting on the porch when Lydia-Ann told Becca the awful news. "I'm moving away," she said. "To Mississippi."

Becca shook her head. "No-sir-ree!" she said. "I won't let you."

A week later Becca was still shaking her head at the Harrisons' Everything-Goes yard sale.

"No-sir-ree!" she said. "I won't buy anything. You need all this stuff because you're staying right here."

Best friends don't move to Mississippi, Becca had decided.

Best friends play king and queen and knights of the Round Table in Lydia-Ann's loft.

Best friends hunt for treasure on the mystery trail behind Becca's house.

And best friends laze around with Midnight Moon, Lydia-Ann's cat, who is always begging for a scratch.

But best friends absolutely, positively, without a doubt do not move to Mississippi.

When moving morning arrived, Becca's head felt as if fireworks were shooting off inside. But she was still shaking it as the Harrison family loaded up the stuff that hadn't gone into the Haul-It-Yourself trailer.

"No-sir-ree!" she muttered to herself. "I won't say good-bye."

Becca wasn't the only one upset. Midnight Moon's tail was swishing faster than a cow's tail zapping flies. He was fixing for a headlong leap into the woods.

"Shoo!" Becca whispered. "Go on, Midnight Moon, scoot!"

Maybe a cat hunt would run some sense into the Harrisons' heads. Maybe they'd give up this Mississippi moving idea.

But Lydia-Ann noticed the tail, too. "Midnight Moon," she scolded, "don't even think about it!"

"Put him in the car," Mr. Harrison said. "We're ready to hit the road."

Lydia-Ann grabbed Becca, hugged her, and cried a little. "Please say good-bye, Becca," she begged.

"No-sir-ree!" Becca said. She watched the Harrisons chug off, car dragging, trailer bouncing.

Best friends don't move to Mississippi! How could she? Why, Lydia-Ann had even given Becca her nickname.

Becca was born Rebecca, but she got tired of it. "Too many Rebeccas," she said. "Rebecca here, Rebecca there, Rebecca everywhere."

So one day Becca made up her mind. "Call me Milly or Tilly or anything you want," she told her friends and family. "Anything but Rebecca."

For three weeks she refused to come when her mother called, "Rebecca, time for supper."

She pretended to be daydreaming when her father said, "Please pass the potatoes, Rebecca."

And at school she wouldn't even crack a smile when Mr. Kline asked, "How's my favorite Rebecca this morning?"

Tempers were frazzled until Lydia-Ann finally got an idea.

"Call yourself Becca," she said.

"Perfect," said Becca. "No other Beccas!"

And there were no other Lydia-Anns.

Best friend Lydia-Ann, who *did* move to Mississippi after all.

Where was Mississippi anyhow? Becca didn't even know.

So when Grandpa Jake offered to take her there for a visit she said, "YES-sir-ree!"

Friday afternoon they started out. They drove all the rest of that day and part of the next.

Finally Becca saw the Harrisons' station wagon.

"Hey, Mississippi," she hollered. "I'm here!"

Becca and Lydia-Ann got right down to business. They had two months' worth of playing to get done in two days.

That meant no stopping until bedtime, when Grandpa Jake told them story after story.

Still, sleeping came hard. It seemed like a waste of time when there was so much for best friends to do.

There was Midnight Moon begging for a scratch.

Potatoes to peel for soup.

And a rickety old shed hiding secrets galore.

For those two glorious days it was like old times again. Old times in a new place.

Then Monday morning came. The girls hugged each other and Lydia-Ann cried a little.

So did Becca.

"Best friends who move to Mississippi," she said, "are so far away . . ." Her voice trailed off.

Lydia-Ann nodded. "No more next-door friends," she said. "Now we're long-distance ones."

Becca shook her head. "You're still next door!" she said. "In my heart."

She pounded Lydia-Ann on the shoulder. "Got you last!" she shouted as she raced to the car and locked the door.

"Just you wait." Lydia-Ann pressed her nose flat against the glass. "I'll get you at Christmas."

Becca laughed and shook her head. "No-sir-ree!" she said.

The Creaky Cure

By Betty Bates

Grandpa hobbled into the kitchen. He hung his cane over the back of his chair and slowly lowered himself into it, his bones as creaky as the cellar door.

"Grandpa," I said, "it's your birthday. You ought to have a party."

"No, Simon. I'm too old to have a birthday party."

"Then how about a quiet and restful *un*birthday party, Grandpa?"

"An *un*birthday party? Hm." He tipped his chair back and snapped his suspenders. "All right," he said at last. "But you'll have to manage it. I'm not up to doing that."

"Okay, Grandpa. You ask the guests, and I'll run the party. That will be my unbirthday present."

Grandpa invited Miss Pattershot from across the creek and Mr. Trimm from across the county road. "Remember, Simon. No gifts in fancy paper, no funny hats, and no frisky games."

That was all right with me. We wouldn't play the usual birthday games like musical chairs. I'd think up just one calm and restful one.

My dog, Scruffy, followed me into the cellar, where I found a green ribbon in Grandpa's Christmas box. I'd use it in my quiet and restful game.

Mr. Trimm came with his fiddle under his arm. "For my unbirthday present," he said, "I'll play you a tune."

"Appreciate it," said Grandpa.

Miss Pattershot had on her dancing shoes. "For my unbirthday present," she said, "I'll do you a dance."

I held up the green ribbon. "Our quiet and restful game is tie-the-ribbon-on-Scruffy. Whoever makes the prettiest bow at his neck with this ribbon is the winner."

Mr. Trimm went first. Scruffy hid under the skirt of Grandpa's easy chair. Mr. Trimm got on his hands and knees and tried to get hold of Scruffy's paws, but Scruffy kept squirming. The rest of us couldn't help chuckling. Finally, Mr. Trimm sighed, scratched his chin, and joined in our chuckles. "That's some stubborn dog," he said, walking away.

Scruffy came out from under the chair. I think he was grinning.

"He just needs coaxing," said Miss Pattershot. "Let me try." She took the ribbon. "Here, Scruffy, dear." Scruffy backed away, and she followed on her plump legs. "It's all right, Scruffy. Such a pretty ribbon." Scruffy only backed up some more, while she pleaded, "Pleeease, Scruffy dear."

But Scruffy wouldn't stop.

We couldn't help giggling. Finally, Miss Pattershot threw up her hands and giggled, too. "I give up," she said.

"I'll show you how," said Grandpa, taking the ribbon. As he hooked his cane over the arm of his chair, Scruffy ran into the hall. Grandpa chased after him. Scruffy scampered through the hall and back into the parlor. He circled around and around, bumping chair legs and mussing rugs. Grandpa dashed after him with the ribbon streaming out behind him.

Those two were fall-down funny. Mr. Trimm laughed so hard he kept slapping his knee. Miss Patterhsot laughed so hard she shook all over. I laughed so hard I hurt. Grandpa laughed so hard he huffed and puffed as he ran.

I think Scruffy was laughing, too.

At last Grandpa gave up. With a last guffaw, he collapsed on the loveseat. When he had caught his breath, he turned to me. "You try it, Simon."

Scruffy hid under the tall wooden legs of the antique highboy.

I went to the kitchen and found last night's ham bone. I set it in Scruffy's dish, brought the dish into the parlor, and laid it in front of the highboy. Scruffy's nose came out first. Then his eyes. Then his ears. Then all of him was out, and he gnawed the bone. I slipped the ribbon around his neck and tied an enormous bow. Miss Pattershot, Mr. Trimm, and Grandpa applauded and cheered. Grandpa cheered the loudest.

I tried to look modest.

"Now," I said, "It's calm and restful gift time."

Mr. Trimm picked up his fiddle. "We ought to call my ungift musical chair," he said.

"Musical *chair?*" asked Grandpa.

"You'll see." Mr. Trimm set his foot smack in the middle of the caned seat of the rocking chair, tucked his fiddle under his chin, and swung into "Skip to My Lou."

The chair rocked back and forth in time to the lively music.

Scruffy rolled over and over, squashing his bow.

I found myself clapping in rhythm.

And Miss Pattershot began to dance a two-step. Her skirt flared, and her dancing shoes *rap-rapped* as she twirled.

Grandpa's foot was tapping. He stood up, and his legs carried him to Miss Pattershot. He swung her around and around, faster and faster, lifting his feet high and banging them on the floor.

With Mr. Trimm fiddling, the chair rocking, Scruffy rolling, me clapping, Miss Pattershot rapping, and Grandpa banging, there was an awful racket.

Mr. Trimm kept playing. He played so hard his foot broke through the seat of the musical chair. Grandpa would have to mend it in the morning.

But as he two-stepped past me with Miss Pattershot, Grandpa didn't appear to care. He didn't seem to need his cane. And he didn't creak. "By cracky, Simon," he shouted over the music, "we ought to do this more often."

I didn't say a word. I just kept clapping.

But I was grinning all over.

The
Dancing Bear
and the
Princess

By Mary Katz

Becky jumped up from her desk. "But I want to be the dancing bear!" she said.

"You're too small to be the bear," said Bobby.

"So why can't it be a small bear?" asked Becky. "Bears aren't all the same size, you know!"

"Everybody calm down," Miss Waterton said. "Becky is right—some bears *are* small. But the bear costume we have is a big one—much too large for Becky, I'm afraid."

"I could make it fit," Becky said.

"I'm sure you could," said Miss Waterton. "But when we borrowed the costumes we had to promise not to cut or sew them."

"OK," Bobby continued, "then Becky will be the princess. We won't have to worry about finding a little bitty costume—the princess just wears a pretty dress and this crown."

As Becky glared at Bobby, she heard a sigh behind her. She turned to see Sheila looking longingly at the sparkling crown.

"Now," said Bobby, "let's have Sheila for the dancing bear. OK, Sheila?"

Sheila sighed again. "I guess so," she said. "The costume will probably fit me."

"Unless it's too small," someone across the room whispered. Sheila slumped down in her seat, and her cheeks turned red. She was the tallest person in the class.

"I don't think I can dance like a bear," she said.

"I know just how bears dance!" Becky jumped up again. "Why not let Sheila be the princess, and let me be the bear?"

"Oh, I would love to be the princess!" Sheila exclaimed.

"Come on, you two," Bobby said. "You know that the bear can't be smaller than the princess! That's totally ridiculous."

"Let's not argue," said Miss Waterton. Becky and Sheila looked at each other. Sheila shrugged and stared down at her desk.

Becky said nothing more. But she kept thinking there had to be a way she could get to be the dancing bear.

When the bell rang, she grabbed Sheila's arm as she passed. "Wait, Sheila," she said. "I want you to come with me to talk to Miss Waterton."

"What are you going to do?" asked Sheila.

"I don't know yet," Becky replied. They waited until the rest of the class had left, then went up to the teacher's desk.

"Miss Waterton?" began Becky.

"Yes, Becky." Miss Waterton looked up.

"Could Sheila and I have just a few minutes tomorrow to convince the class that we should trade parts?"

"Why is this so important to you girls?" asked Miss Waterton. "You both have nice parts for the play, and you'll be good in those roles."

Sheila blushed and looked at her feet, but Becky was determined. "It's important to me," she said, "because I'm tired of people thinking I can't do some things just because I'm small."

"Do you feel the same way, Sheila?" asked Miss Waterton gently.

"Well, sort of," said Sheila. "I hate being the tallest because everyone teases me and makes me feel ugly."

Miss Waterton was quiet for a moment. "I'll certainly be glad to give you a chance to prove your point," she said slowly. "But, Becky," she added, "I don't see how you can possibly make the bear costume fit."

"I'll find a way," Becky said. "May I take it home with me tonight?"

"Only if you'll promise not to damage it," Miss Waterton said.

"I promise!" Becky said. "And if I can't make it fit, Sheila and I will keep the parts we have and not say anything else about it. Right, Sheila?"

"I guess," Sheila said. "I just know I'll end up being the clunky old bear anyway, and everyone will laugh at me."

"Oh, come on, Sheila," Becky said. "You're going to be the princess!"

"I hope so," she said, still discouraged.

Becky hurried home with the bear costume in a paper bag. Sheila was coming over as soon as she could. Becky ran through the kitchen and up the stairs. She pulled the bundle of fuzzy brown cloth out of the bag, struggled into the costume, and stood in front of her mirror. The arms hung down way past her hands and she was walking on the bottoms of the legs.

Looking at her small body, almost lost in the baggy brown fur, Becky began to feel discouraged. "Maybe I am too little after all," she said to herself with a sigh.

Slowly, an idea came to her. She reached down and pulled one fuzzy leg up. Then she slipped her foot back into one of the tall brown boots she had worn to school. Tucking the leg of the costume into it, Becky zipped the boot up. Then she adjusted the costume leg until it brushed the top of her foot.

"This just might work," she said out loud. Quickly, she put on the other boot. "I think I can stuff all this extra sleeve into my mittens," she said, looking in the mirror again. She pulled on woolly, brown mittens. Now the legs and sleeves looked all right, but the body was still too big and baggy.

Just then the doorbell rang and Becky ran downstairs. When she opened the door and Sheila saw the baggy costume, she laughed and said, "That looks like my dad's Santa suit before he stuffs it with pillows!"

"Pillows!" shouted Becky. "Come on, Sheila!" She raced upstairs. Sheila followed, carrying a long, yellow dress.

Becky stuffed soft pillows into the bear suit. In the mirror, she saw a fuzzy bear with a plump body and stubby arms and legs.

Sheila put on the yellow dress. Then she practiced walking gracefully, like an elegant princess.

The next day at school the class was surprised when Miss Waterton said, "We're going to talk some more about the parts for the play. Becky and Sheila, you may get ready now."

The girls rushed out of the room. A few minutes later an elegant, tall princess and a short, plump bear came back. The princess glided gracefully to her throne. The bear rushed up to her and growled ferociously. The princess looked very frightened. But then the bear backed away, made a little curtsy, and shuffled around in a dance. The class laughed and clapped.

"Now," said Miss Waterton with a smile, "does anyone object to Becky playing the bear or Sheila being the princess?"

There were no objections, and Becky and Sheila grinned at each other. The small bear and the tall princess bowed to their audience and happily left the room together.

How Do You Hide a Violin?

By Eve Bunting

Tom walked quickly along the street. He was on his way to his music lesson. His black violin case bumped against his knee. He walked as fast as he could. And he hoped and hoped that he wouldn't meet any of the kids.

The kids in his old school were always putting him down. Tom couldn't understand why they thought it was funny that a boy played violin. Did they think music was only for girls? Anyway, he was glad that the kids here didn't know yet.

Then he saw Clint Carson coming around the corner. Clint Carson! Of all the boys he didn't want to meet.

Tom had spotted Clint in class the first day. He could tell that Clint was an important person in the sixth grade. He was always picked first for the playground games. And Tom had seen *C. Carson* listed as captain of tonight's baseball game.

Now Clint was going to see Tom with a violin. Tom wished he played flute. You could hide a flute. But how could you hide a violin?

The best way was to hide yourself with it. Tom hid behind the shrubbery until Clint passed.

"Did you have a good lesson?" his mom asked him that night at dinner.

"It was OK," Tom said.

"Do you like your new teacher?"

"She's OK." Tom pushed his meat loaf around on his plate. "I'm thinking of stopping violin."

"What?" His mom stared across the table. "But you love violin."

"I know," he said. He did love it. Running the bow across the strings. Hearing the sounds of his own music.

"Oh heck!" He pushed back his chair. "Is it OK if I go to the baseball game? It's just across in the park. It will be over by eight or so."

"All right." His mom looked dazed. *She's probably still thinking about my violin,* Tom thought.

He walked slowly across to the park. Sometimes life was a bummer!

Kids sat around on benches and on the grass. Tom sat by himself under a tree. He wished he weren't shy. He wished he could sit with the rest of the kids and say, "What's happening?" or "How's it going?" But he just couldn't.

Some of the players were already on the field throwing the ball around. The game would be starting soon.

Someone plopped down beside Tom. It was Clint Carson.

"Hi," Clint said. "I've seen you around. Don't you live in the Rayburn Apartments? That's on the corner of my street."

"Right," Tom said. "I've seen you around, too." Suddenly he realized something. Clint Carson was here. Not on the baseball field. "Aren't you playing?" he asked. "I saw your name on the notice board."

"*C.* Carson," Clint said. "That's my sister Cathy. She's team captain. And that's pretty good. She's only in fifth grade."

"Your sister!"

"Yes." Clint was staring at him. "I wanted to ask you. Do you play violin? Somebody said you did."

Tom felt his stomach drop. Here it was again. What if he said "no"? He could lie. He opened his mouth, but the word stuck in his throat. "Yes," he said, quietly.

Clint smiled. "Hey! That's terrific. I play bass. You're lucky you only have to lug a violin around. That bass is a pain."

Tom swallowed. "It must be hard to hide a bass," he said.

"What?" Clint asked.

"Nothing."

"Are you going to try out for orchestra?" Clint asked. "We're pretty good. If you like, you can come to my house, and I'll show you some of the pieces we play."

Their team was running out on the field. Tom cheered with Clint.

"If you come over tomorrow, you can probably eat dinner with us," Clint said. "I'll ask. Tomorrow's my dad's turn to cook. Come early and we can both help him."

They didn't talk any more till the end of the inning. Then Clint asked, "What did you mean, it must be hard to hide a bass?"

"Oh, nothing," Tom said. "Who needs to hide a bass? Or a violin? Or anything?"

Good News for Jagat

By Mildred H. Tengbom

"*Namaste!*" Jagat called the greeting to his friend, the Lady Doctor, standing in the doorway of the hospital.

The Lady Doctor returned his smile. "*Namaste,* Jagat. Where are you off to?"

"To enroll in school. I've got to hurry. It might be too late."

"What happened?"

"Father and I made a trip to get our year's supply of salt. We just got back last night. We didn't know the school would be ready so soon."

"Run, then," the doctor laughed. "You might catch up with Maila on the way."

"Good-bye!" Jagat called as he ran down the path rolling his hoop.

Twenty years ago nobody in Jagat's village in Nepal knew how to read. Many hadn't even seen a book. And now he, Jagat, son of Basant, was going to get a chance to go to school! Maybe he would become a famous doctor. He would put people to sleep, cut them open, and take out whatever was making them sick. Then they would be well again. Jagat threw his hoop into the air and caught it with his stick.

An airplane roared overhead. Jagat stopped to watch. Maybe he could become a pilot, swooping in and out among the Himalayan Mountains up among the clouds.

And then he saw Maila on the trail ahead. Maila, dragging one leg.

Jagat ran up to him. "Where are you going?" he asked without thinking. It was the customary greeting of his people when they met each other on the way. Then Jagat laughed and answered for himself, "But I know where you are going, and I'm going, too. Won't it be fun?" And the boys walked on together, talking about all the exciting things that lay in store for them.

The headmaster had set up a table and chairs in the yard.

"We've come to write our names to read in the school," Jagat explained.

The headmaster shook his head sadly. "But two of you come together. I have only one place left, and now which name shall I write?"

Jagat looked at Maila, and Maila looked at Jagat.

"You're sure there isn't room for both of us?"

"Absolutely sure." The headmaster's eyes were tired. He spread his hands out in front of him helplessly. "I shall have to think about this matter. Come back tomorrow, and I shall tell you whose name I have written."

The boys walked away. Maila seemed to limp more than ever. Jagat looped his hoop over his stick and carried it. Maybe he wouldn't be able to go to school after all.

At home Jagat picked up his slingshot. "I'm going to guard the fields against the birds," he called to his mother as he headed down the trail.

In the fields Jagat turned his problem over and over in his mind. Could his father talk to the headmaster? Or the Lady Doctor? But then he remembered how the Lady Doctor had said to him, "If anyone needs to go to school and learn a trade, it's Maila."

He had asked the Lady Doctor once about Maila's leg. She had said that she couldn't operate on it, but she had a doctor friend who could. He was far away, though, and it would cost lots of money to get Maila there.

Jagat felt all mixed up. He wanted to go to school. And Maila also wanted to go to school. But there was room for only one.

The sun was hot. Jagat was tired. And trying to find a solution for his problem made his head ache. He lay down and soon was fast asleep.

He dreamed. In his dream he was a beggar sitting on a sidewalk. Throngs of people passed him. Some stopped to give him a coin or two. But most of them walked right past. Then he felt a hand on his shoulder. A police officer was shaking him. "Clear out of here. Don't you know it's against the law to beg?"

"Jagat! Wake up! Your mother and I have been hunting for you."

Jagat opened his eyes to see the stars twinkling overhead. Why, it was his father. He jumped up, then remembered, and looked down at his legs. They both were good. He said nothing but quietly followed his father home.

A serious little boy stood before the headmaster the next morning.

"I have good news for you, Jagat," the head-master began. "Several people tell me that you learn quickly, that you are reliable, and work hard. I believe you should be given the chance."

For a moment Jagat wanted to say, "Oh, thank you," and run home with the good news.

But then he remembered the words of the Lady Doctor. One day when he had been watching her in the clinic, he had asked her why she had left her own people to come to his land to work with his people.

The Lady Doctor had smiled that radiant smile of hers as she answered simply, "Because I wanted you to be happy, Jagat."

How many times Jagat had puzzled over that answer, which came back to him now. More than anything else, he guessed, he wanted Maila to be happy. He drew in a long breath and squarely faced the headmaster.

"Thank you. It is kind of you. But I want Maila to have the chance."

The headmaster dropped his papers in astonishment. He opened his mouth, then closed it again. He looked closely at Jagat. Then he asked, "Are you sure you mean this?"

Jagat nodded his head. "Sure," he answered and walked out the door.

I should feel happy, Jagat thought. But he didn't. He heard the roar of a plane above him. Maybe he never would be able to fly a plane or become a doctor and make people well. The thought was more than he could bear. He slumped down behind a bush and cried.

The sound of someone coming down the path made him rub his eyes and nose dry on his sleeve. It was the Lady Doctor. Jagat stepped out onto the path and waited.

"Why, Jagat, *namaste!*" she cried in surprise, waving a letter. "Good news! My doctor friend has written that they have a fund available for Maila's trip. So I will take him there for his operation at once. And, Jagat," she stooped down and gave him a quick hug, "the best news of all is that there is a school for children right in the hospital. Maila will learn while he is there."

"Wonderful!" Jagat's eyes were getting all wet as he expressed it. "Then Maila will be happy."

And he wanted to add, "Do you know what? Now I, too, will get a chance to go to school. Maybe I'll be a doctor after all." Instead, he just smiled at the Lady Doctor and said, "Good-bye. I have to see the headmaster." Happily, he turned and ran back up the path.

A Valentine for Jackie

By Sister Mary Murray, H.M.

"This puppy's mine!" cried Jackie in delight. "Look, Benjamin, he knows me already!" The tiny black puppy was licking her face with his warm, pink tongue.

"Yeah," said Benjamin, grinning.

But Benjamin's other friends paid little attention to Jackie.

"I choose this one!" said Mike. "Maybe if it's small enough, Mother will let me keep it."

"I want a puppy, too," cried one boy after another.

"Sorry, guys, sorry! All the puppies are sold or promised, every one of them," said Benjamin.

Jackie could hardly believe her ears.

"Sold! Or promised!"

To hide the tears that sprang to her eyes, she buried her face in the puppy's soft fur. Then, quickly, she handed the warm little animal to Benjamin and slipped out of the shed.

"Is that you, Jackie?" called her mother, putting her hand over the mouthpiece of the phone. "Change your school clothes before you play."

"Yes, Mother," answered Jackie. The big lump in her throat was choking her.

"Sold or promised! Sold or promised!" Each step she took pounded out those horrible words.

Slowly she opened her treasure box hidden in the closet. She fingered the blue-and-white agate Benjamin had won for her in the marble contest. She played with the white rabbit tail he had told her to keep for good luck. Ever since she could remember, she and Benjamin had been the closest friends. Only last week he had asked her what color dog she liked best. Now that she had chosen the puppy she thought was meant for her, Benjamin had only tossed his head. "Sorry, guys, sorry! All the puppies are sold or promised—yes, every one of them!" Those nasty words!

74

Suddenly Jackie threw herself on the bed and burst into tears. She sobbed so hard she could feel the bed shake. Little rivers of water trickled down the corners of her pillow. Finally, she felt a cool, gentle hand on her forehead.

"Why, Jackie, whatever is the matter?" asked her mother kindly.

"Nothing, Mother, nothing!" sobbed Jackie. "But I'm never going to play with Benjamin again. Never!"

Little by little, Jackie blurted out her disappointment and the way Benjamin had hurt her feelings.

"Now, Jackie," said her mother. "Did Benjamin really promise you a puppy? He doesn't have to give you one, you know."

"I know, Mother. But, oh, how I wanted that puppy. And he wanted me, too. I could tell."

"I'll tell you what, Jackie. Cora's valentine party is just a few days away. Perhaps we could manage a new dress for the party. Perhaps even enough valentines for your classmates. Let's shop after school tomorrow. How about it?"

"I'd love that, Mother," said Jackie. "But I won't buy a valentine for Benjamin. He'll never get one from me again. He'll never get anything from me ever again!"

Jackie spent Saturday afternoon signing valentines. Then she read and reread each one. "Look,

Mother, at this one for Cora," she said. "It is a valentine thank-you for her party."

"*A thank-you to my friend,*" Mother read. "It's lovely, Jackie. I'm sure Cora will like it."

At school right after lunch on Valentine's Day, Jackie was chosen to open the class valentine box decorated with red and white hearts. Then she chose six postmen to deliver the valentines.

"Cora is not here this afternoon," said Miss Hart. "You may put her valentines on my desk."

Jackie counted as each valentine fell on her desk. "Twenty-three," she counted. "And there are twenty-five in the class. I know who didn't send me one." She felt her face grow warm. She looked at the names on each one of her cards to keep from crying. Yes, she was correct. There was no card from Benjamin. Well, this really ended their friendship.

Finally, the dismissal bell rang. Then Miss Hart said, "I'm sorry to have to announce this. Cora Gables has the measles. Her party will have to be postponed for a while. Also I would like to have some helpers for a few minutes after school."

"I'll help," said Jackie.

Jackie walked home slowly. Why should she hurry? No party! No valentine! At least, not the one she wanted.

When she opened the front door, the younger children came running to her. "Valentine!" they cried. "Jackie got a valentine."

"Hi, Cupid!" teased her older brother. "It's in your room."

"I'd say it's a very special valentine," said her mother with a twinkle in her eye.

Jackie could not believe her eyes. On her bed stood a large valentine box much like the one in school. On its side in red and white tiny hearts were the words "A Valentine for Jackie." Her heart skipped a beat. She ran to the box.

"Yap! Yap!" barked a tiny black puppy. Jackie lifted it gently from the box and hugged it.

"Read the note, Jackie! It's tied to the ribbon," said her mother.

Jackie read aloud:

> *Dear Jackie:*
> *I wanted to come to you sooner. But this is the first day I could leave my mother. Please be good to me.*
>  *Your Valentine*

"Oh, Mother," said Jackie. "What will I do about Benjamin? I didn't give him a valentine."

"I did!" said her older brother. "Wasn't the thank-you valentine for Benjamin? It was on the table. Anyhow, he has it now."

"Yes, yes, it was," said Jackie. "Very definitely it was!" She winked at her mother. "I can get another card for Cora's party."

The
Black
Top Hat

By Scott K. Miller

Early one morning in New York City, Treat and his friend Erica left the apartment building where they lived and walked over to Central Park.

"It sure is windy today," Treat said, as he pulled his baseball cap down tight on his head.

"It sure is," Erica agreed. "I like windy days; it makes the city smell fresh and clean."

Treat smiled at his friend. She could always find something good in everything. Treat was glad that Erica's family had moved into the same apartment building in which his family lived. In no time at all, they had become good friends.

Soon they were at Central Park. Even though it was early in the morning, the city's biggest park was already alive with people.

"I hope all the swings are not taken already," Treat said with a frown.

"Maybe not," Erica said. "It's still early."

Together, they hurried down the carriage path that led to the playground swings. The trees that lined the path dipped and swayed in the wind. Suddenly, Erica stopped. "Treat, look at that," she said in surprise. Tumbling along the path was a hat—a black top hat.

"Come on!" Treat yelled.

Treat and Erica raced after the hat. They caught it before it blew away.

"Gee, what a nice hat. I wonder who could have lost it?" Erica said. "It looks like a magician's hat."

"Maybe there's a rabbit inside it," Treat said with a chuckle. Erica laughed, too.

"You know, Treat, not very many people wear top hats. I bet we could find the owner if we tried."

Treat thought of the swings at the playground.

"Oh, Erica, there are millions of people in New York City. I don't think we could ever find the owner of this hat."

"Well, if you lost your baseball cap, wouldn't you want someone to return it to you?"

"Yes, I would, but . . ." Treat saw the determined look on Erica's face.

"All right," Treat finally said.

Treat and Erica began to walk all around the park, looking for someone who might have lost a top hat. They asked a man who was selling hot dogs from a pushcart.

"Hot dogs! Get your hot dogs here!" the man yelled, trying to attract customers.

"Excuse me, sir," Treat said politely. "Have you seen anyone who might have lost this hat?"

"No," the man said. "Would you like to buy a hot dog?"

"No, thank you," Treat said disappointedly.

Next, they stopped and asked a man selling bright-colored balloons. The man just shook his head no. "I'll tell you what," the man said. "I will trade you one of my balloons for the hat." This time, Treat and Erica shook their heads.

"No, thank you," Erica said. "We don't want to trade our hat."

Treat and Erica walked some more. They saw joggers and bicyclists and other kinds of people, but no one who might have lost a black top hat.

Finally, they sat on a park bench to rest.

"You were right, Treat," Erica said. "I guess we will never find the owner of this hat. And all the swings must be taken by now."

Just then, Treat spied a police officer walking through the park on her beat. "Look, Erica," Treat said, "maybe that police officer can help us."

"Excuse me, Officer," Treat said politely. "We found this hat blowing in the wind. Have you seen anyone who might have lost it?"

"Hmmm," the police officer said, scratching her head. "The only people I have ever seen wearing top hats in the park are cab drivers." Treat and Erica were puzzled.

"A cab driver?" Erica asked. "What kind of cab driver wears a top hat?" For an instant, Treat and Erica stared at each other with their mouths open wide. "Oh! A *hansom* cab driver!" they cried. Together, they thanked the officer and hurried off toward the 59th Street entrance.

On the street outside the park were five hansom cabs—horsedrawn carriages that looked as though they would be fun to ride in. As Treat and Erica walked along the row of cabs, their hearts sank. They could see that every cab driver had on a top hat. Now they did not know what to do.

Suddenly, Erica heard something. "What's that?" she said. Over the noise of the city traffic, Treat and Erica could hear the *clip-clop, clip-clop* of a horse's hoofs coming around the corner.

"Look, Treat!" Erica said, as a hansom cab came into view. "That cab driver has no hat."

"Hello, Mister," Treat called. Erica held the black top hat high in the air for the driver to see.

"Oh, you found my hat," he said. "It blew off my head in the park, and by the time I stopped my cab and jumped down, it had blown away. I thought it was gone for good."

Erica handed the man his top hat. "We were on our way to the playground swings and found it blowing along the carriage path," she said.

"Thank you very much," the man said happily. "It was kind of you to take the time to find me."

"We're glad that we were able to find you," Treat said.

"You were on your way to the playground swings?" the man asked.

"Yes, we were," Treat said.

"How would you like to ride to the playground in my carriage?" asked the man, as he placed the top hat on his head.

"I've never ridden in a hansom cab," Erica said.

"Neither have I," Treat added.

The cab driver took the reins in his hands. "Well then, climb aboard," he said.

Treat and Erica were so excited they could hardly believe it. Treat took Erica by the hand and helped her into the carriage. Then he climbed in next to her. The cab driver snapped the reins. "Giddap," he called to the horse. The hansom cab moved slowly through the park. Treat and Erica waved to all the people they passed along the way. At the playground, much to their surprise, two swings stood empty waiting for them.

Recipe for a Tough Cookie

By Margaret Walden Froehlich

Julius "Wimp" Peterson gets picked on by everybody because he is such a namby-pamby, whiney-fuss baby of an eight-year-old boy. Take it from me. I've been baby-sitting with him after school since I was eleven and he was five. I have to say, though, that I really like the poor kid.

One afternoon about two weeks before Halloween, Wimp came home from school with a bloody lip. "Look what T.G. Knapp and Danny and Marianne did to me today, Dorcas," he bawled.

As a rule Wimp is the color of skim milk and as scrawny as a long-dead mouse. His eyes are red-rimmed from crying, and his pale hair could stand cream rinse with conditioner to give it added body. The latest decoration on his face didn't do a thing for him.

"Wimp, they pick on you because you're such a scaredy-cat. If you were brave, they'd leave you alone," I said, giving him a consoling hug. "Halloween is coming, and I have an idea how we can prove to those kids that you're one tough cookie.

"You know that so-called haunted house over on Cherry Street?" I continued. "Anybody who would go trick-or-treating over there on Halloween night would be pretty brave, huh? Anybody who would go right up to the door and stand there when a monster opened it and maybe punch the monster right in the nose would be super-colossal brave, wouldn't he?"

Wimp was staring at me with his mouth wide open. "Dorcas," he finally gasped, "are you kidding me?"

"No, I am not kidding," I said. "Listen, I know for a fact that that house is *not* haunted because I've been there a lot of times with my mother when she takes meals to old Mrs. Barry who lives there. I'm going to ask Mrs. Barry if I can borrow her front hall on Halloween night to help out a friend in need."

"I'll dress up in something scary and wait in Mrs. Barry's front hall for you and those second-grade bullies to come along trick-or-treating. You walk up to the door bold as brass because you know it's just me in there, and you bang on the door and yell, 'Trick or treat!' I'll yank the door open, and you can sock me in the nose. Got it?"

"Wimp, I'll turn you into the bravest guy in the second grade. Those kids will never lay a finger on you again."

Wimp and I set the plan in motion the next day. He went off to school with instructions to begin bragging that he was going trick-or-treating at the haunted house.

On the twenty-ninth I offered to take Mrs. Barry's supper to her, and I took Wimp with me.

"Here's my friend-in-need, Mrs. Barry," I said, introducing Wimp. Wimp looked a little nervous, but he said, "Thank you," when Mrs. Barry gave him the little package of crackers that went with her soup.

"Dorcas is a fine young lady," Mrs. Barry said.

"She baby-sits with me," Wimp said. "She's turning me into the bravest kid in the second grade, so I won't get beat up all the time." Then the three of us discussed exactly how we would carry out my plan.

The next afternoon Wimp and I rigged green cellophane over the lens of a flashlight, figuring that some green light would make Mrs. Barry's house look really haunted. I showed him my costume—an old black suit that I had found in the attic, a fuzzy wig that belonged to my mother, a stocking, and a red marker for blood.

"Dorcas, that stuff isn't scary," Wimp complained.

"You're disappointed, huh?" I said. "Did you notice that I have only one stocking here and that I have two legs?"

"Dorcas, you're gooney," Wimp said.

"OK, old buddy, now watch and remember that it's just me, gooney old Dorcas, your baby-sitter, under here." I stretched the stocking and pulled it down over my face, squashing my ordinarily attractive nose.

From behind the couch Wimp called in a voice that was too high-pitched, "You're gooney, Dorcas!"

I yanked off the stocking, saying, "Ta-dah! Just gooney old Dorcas under here." Wimp came out from behind the couch.

On Halloween night I walked him to the firehouse where there was a party for the kids and where Wimp was supposed to meet Danny and

Marianne and T.G. Figuring that the fire fighters would never let T.G. drown Wimp in the apple-bobbing tub, I lit out for Mrs. Barry's to get ready.

I was hiding in the hall, squirting green light out through the narrow windows on either side of the door, when I heard T.G.'s voice from outside. "He's gonna chicken out! I know he is!"

Then there was a feeble tap on the front door, and in the silence that followed, I heard Wimp bleat, "Trick or treat!"

I swirled the light around and then yanked open the creaking door, holding the flashlight so that it would shine on my squashed face. The sharp upper-cut caught me unawares, and the flashlight clattered to the porch floor. T.G. and his buddies vanished screaming into the night.

I pulled Wimp inside with a hug and lifted his skinny arm in the air. "Julius Peterson, the winner! Hooray for the Tough Cookie!"

"You didn't scare me even for a minute, Dorcas," he said. He dove into his trick-or-treat bag and came up with two candy bars. "Here," he said. "One for you and one for Mrs. Barry." The kid had a smug look on his face that I had never seen before. I wondered for a minute if I had let a genie out of its bottle. I only hoped I wouldn't regret it.

Kirsten Comes Out of Her Shell

By Lorrie McLaughlin

Kirsten walked slowly into the schoolyard. The other girls were already standing around in little groups, laughing and talking. She hesitated by the steps, wishing she had courage enough to join one of the groups. School in this strange new country wasn't so bad when she could sit at her desk, head hidden behind an open book. She didn't feel so much out of things then.

"If only we could have stayed in Denmark," she thought for the hundredth time. Things had been so different there. She had been the center of a friendly group of girls, and she hadn't had to struggle to learn a new language and new ways.

Just before school ended for the day, Miss Coghill, the teacher, announced, "I have a special surprise today. The school is going to have a Fun Fair to raise money for playground equipment. We are dividing the class into small groups. Each group will be responsible for a booth at the fair."

Kirsten waited breathlessly. Now she would be part of a group!

"Connie Labar, Kirsten Lacour, Jennie Larsen," read Miss Coghill, "will make up one group."

Kirsten went timidly toward Jennie and Connie who sat together at the front of the room. "I am with you?" she asked.

"I suppose so," Connie replied, quickly turning to Jennie. "We've got to think of something special for the Fun Fair, Jen."

"Please," said Kirsten, "I want to help, but what is a Fun Fair?"

"You mean you haven't even heard of a Fun Fair?" asked Jennie.

Kirsten shook her head.

"Well, it's a sort of sale," Jennie explained. "There are games, and people sell things like candy and white elephants."

Kirsten gasped. "Now you are joking!"

"Oh, Kirsten," laughed Jennie. "A white elephant is something you don't want any more—like a book you've read or a doll or a vase."

"I see," Kirsten said doubtfully.

"I guess it's going to be up to you and me to do the work on this booth, Jennie," said Connie crossly. "Kirsten won't be any help at all if she has to have every little thing explained to her."

"That's not fair, Connie," said Jennie. "Kirsten can't help it if she doesn't know about a Fun Fair."

"I will go out of the group if you like," Kirsten offered quietly.

"You will not!" said Jennie. "You're part of the class, and you're in our group."

"Well, I'm not," said Connie. "I'm going to ask Miss Coghill to let me join another group." And she stamped away.

"Now you are almost alone," said Kirsten sadly. "You have just me and I am next to no good at all."

"You're fine," said Jennie, but her eyes were on Connie. "Connie just likes to be best at everything," she apologized.

"She is not best at being a friend," said Kirsten earnestly. "You are that."

By the end of the week, the two girls still had no plans. "It's harder than I thought," Jennie admitted to Kirsten as the two girls walked slowly home from school. "Every time we think of something, we find out one of the other groups had the idea first. Kirsten, can't you think of anything?"

Kirsten shook her head sadly. "It is hard to think of an idea for something so strange. If you asked, Connie would let you join her group," she added.

Jennie shook her head. "We'll just have to put on our thinking caps and come up with something really good."

Kirsten frowned. "You have so many strange words," she said. "Thinking cap—what is that?"

Jennie laughed. "Oh, Kirsten, how hard a new language must be for you! A thinking cap isn't a real cap. It means we'll have to think extra hard."

When the two girls reached the corner where they usually said good-bye, Kirsten said shyly, "My mother said I should ask you to come home for a glass of milk and some cookies if you want to. But if you are busy, we will understand."

"I'd love to come over, Kirsten," Jennie said quickly. "And tomorrow you come home with me and meet my family."

Kirsten led Jennie into a big, sunny kitchen and introduced her friend to her mother.

"I am very happy," said Mrs. Lacour, in a voice just like Kirsten's. "It is pleasure to meet you."

She set two glasses of milk on the table beside a plate of cookies and little sandwiches.

Jennie ate several of the tiny open sandwiches. "These are delicious," Jennie said to Mrs. Lacour. "I've never tasted anything like them."

"They are great favorites in Denmark," explained Kirsten. "The cookies are Danish, too."

Jennie bit into a cookie. "Mmmm," she said. "It must be hard to cook like this."

Kirsten shook her head. "It is easy. Even I can do it," she giggled, "and you know how stupid I am."

"Not when you come out of your shell!"

"Out of my shell—what is that?"

"That means when you stop being so shy and quiet," explained Jennie. She looked at the cookies and sandwiches again. "Are these really easy to make?" she asked thoughtfully.

Kirsten nodded. Then her eyes widened as she looked at Jennie. "We are both putting on our thinking caps at once!" she said.

"We can sell cookies and sandwiches like these," said Jennie eagerly, "and we can call our booth Little Denmark!"

Kirsten nodded happily. "Excuse me. I'll be right back," she shouted as she ran upstairs.

When she came back she was carrying two dresses, full-skirted and embroidered, and two small lacy caps. She handed one cap to Jennie. "From Denmark we brought these. Mother says we may wear them in the booth."

The night of the Fun Fair, Kirsten and Jennie spread their counter with tiny sandwiches and cookies and tall paper cups of milk. As they waited for their customers to arrive, Connie walked slowly up to the booth.

"You've got the best booth here," she said. "I'm sorry I was horrid the other day. I hope you both will forgive me."

"Of course we do," said Jennie, looking at Kirsten.

Kirsten nodded as she held out a plate of cookies. "Have a sample for luck!"

"It's on the house," Jennie said, laughing. "That means Connie is getting it for free," she explained to Kirsten.

Connie picked up one of the cookies and smiled. "Thanks," she said. "Let's all walk home together after the fair."

Kirsten looked around the crowded room with joy in her heart. For the first time since she'd left Denmark she felt that she was really among friends.